THE SEVENTEENTH SEASON

Published By

The Seventeenth Season

Edited By Christy & Shruti

Published by: Poetry World Org.

Publisher's Address: Haryana

Printed under PWO in India

Edition : I (2022)

ISBN (Paperback) - 9789392507250

Book Design by POETRY WORLD

THE SEVENTEENTH SEASON

Compilers

Christy Gnana Deepa J

Shruti Agarwal

THE SEVENTEENTH SEASON

The Seventeenth Season is an anthology of youth's desires, dreams, and Nostalgic memories of college days. This book talks about the teenage phase an individual goes through and grows through. This phase is unique in everyone's life as they are and this is a ray of nostalgia for every writer. This book is a collection of beautiful anecdotes, poems, and short stories which make the reader's heart frisky and entertaining.

COMPILER

Christy Gnana Deepa, 20, hailing from Tamilnadu, India. Her journey till date is amazing by being a compiler of 5 anthologies and a co-author of more than 45+ anthologies. A writer by passion and a literarian by profession. She posts her writeups on Yourquote, Instagram, and NbliK.

Insta Id- __budding__writer

HOPE & THE END

Signs of Hope! Yes. It all began with hope!

A glimpse of new faces and new smiles,

Pretty new etiquette, Attractive new classroom,

Beautiful caring friends

It's perfectly new! Yes, we relished it, we enjoyed it!

Every beginning has an end. How was your end?

Maybe...

Perfectly Imperfect ending with tears!

Words of consolation, Group of selfies...

What not? Yes, It's the end.

The end of school/ college life!

Christy Gnana Deepa J

COMPILER

Shruti Agarwal, 24, is residing in Rajasthan, India with her family. She has completed her graduation and now she is pursuing the chartered accountancy course (CA). Her inspiration is her mother. She prefers creating content in English and Hindi, her work is multifarious so that every reader could relate to at least one aspect. She believes in "don't stop shining just because someone gets inspired by your light.

Some of her write-ups have been published in Anthologies: Thorny roses, Shining dreams, My mother: My power, The Beautiful love bond, The invisible bond, The Eulogizer, Unique Pieces, Jaayaz Ishq, Supriya-Ek Apsara.

Insta I'd: Shaan_0612.

LOVE YOUR LIFE

You are a human,

It's okay to have some problems,

It's okay to hit rock bottom,

It's okay to have heartbroken,

It's okay to feel negative emotions.

These are just life lessons.

This life belongs to you only,

Make yourself as a priority,

It starts with Loving you selfishly,

Then life will take your dreams seriously.

Your life thinks highly of you,

It looks up only to you,

It believes in infinite opportunities

Then why do you stand steady?

Putting yourself last doesn't make you better,

Putting yourself first is always healthier,

Love yourself to fill your cup first,

And then make this world the happiest.

Be proud of who you are,

Be yourself and shine like the star,

Don't worry about comment's shower,

Love your beauty, embrace this flower.

Shruti Agarwal

ACKNOWLEDGEMENT

We would like to thank the "Poetry world organization" for providing us with this wonderful opportunity of collecting such lovely writers and compiling this book. Furthermore, we would like to thank all the writers for actively participating and making this anthology a successful one. Last but not the least, we would like to thank the Almighty and our family especially our mom who supported and motivated us throughout the course of this project.

INDEX

THE WINGS OF FIRE

Come out with the claws of power,
With immense gusto and foresight,
With severe hunger for success!
Come out with your strong diamond heart,
Maintaining your wisdom and courage,
To quench your thirst of satisfaction!
Come out with your boiling blood,
To free yourself from ignorance,
And break the walls of superstitions!
Come out with a metal strong desire,
To search for the prey of opportunities,
Overcoming the hurdles called situations!
Come out with the wings of fire
To fly towards your destiny,
With an ever-burning desire!
Come out with high voltage power
With a capacity to digest your sorrows,
And fight back the reason behind every drop of your
tear!
Come out with natural acceptance,
Because a powerful eagle you are,
Not just any ordinary bird,
Who hide from rain of problems,
But you can fly above the clouds of difficulties!
To fly about peacefully and daringly,
In the blue sky called life!

PRANAYE RACHAMALLA

JOURNEY OF THE CLAY & POTTER, LIFE AND YOU

You only are the Clay; you only are the Potter,
O, Young Man! You may be scattered today,
In the form of mud, Effete & spread away,
Has no special utility, yet special ductility,
Perceive and know your life as Clay,
Give beautiful shape with Virtues every day;

Attentiveness, humbleness, gratitude, and wisdom,
Equally important culture & consistency
memorandum,
Form and decorate the pitcher of the Life Fathom,
After a long practice, you will become disciplined,
For the future ~ Organized, Planned & Restrained;

Purpose and Goal of your life be the Best,
With Creativity and Focus, Aim it with high Zest,
Exuberance, sparkle, vigor, liveliness sees no rest,
Moments be filled with droplets of success test,
Time bringing happiness, should not go waste,
You will wear a special shape and the special thing:
The potter who shaped you is none other than you
yourself being;

Wheel Axle Water all in one ~ vests & kneads the
Clay,
Parents, teachers and trust in oneself nests & feeds
us faraway,
Fingers and hands define a concise pot,

Routine, practice, friends and senses determine you
a lot,
The outer teachings will only support you,
You have to craft yourself from the unique potential
within you;

External hear -preaching cannot shape you,
A sense of direction it will only give you,
In the present, you may be clay,
But in future you will have to become an assembler,
your own maker, Hey;
You yourself are the sculptor of your life and
upcoming future,
You only are the Clay; you only are the Potter.

RADHIKA BHARTIYA

FIREFLIES OF MEMORIES

Dwelling into the old books, nostalgia caught my
eyes.
Nostalgia, containing the very essence of our college
days, specifically that bench!
That bench which had got our names engraved on it,
undeciphered by all and deciphered by us only.
That bench that had still got our memories
preserved in the deep cracks of its wood.
That bench had broken the shackles of time and
kept our gossip alive in the form of dust.
That bench is still shining brighter and brighter
under the same sun rays,
Under the same rainy clouds, and under the same
dusty winds,
All entering through the holes of that broken
window.
I know, that bench is still craving for getting our
imprints again,
Sharing the memories again,
Letting her taste our lunches again,
Engraving our names on her again.
I know that bench is shining brighter and brighter,
beautified by our memories.
I promise I will surely come to you my dear bench,
For revisiting the lanes of college days
Which you have preserved for us so far.

ANJALI SRIVASTAVA

MY PRICELESS VOYAGE

My Priceless Voyage,
Loaded with dreams,
I entered into my college life.
The trees greeted me,
By shaking its feathers up and down.
And the gentle breeze says,
Good days are impending.
English enticed me into literature,
It connected my soul with nature.
And of course! New companions on my path,
The three years traveled like three seconds.
When I came out, our tracks separated
The next journey started,
With blissful memories.

M. HEMALATHA

COLLEGE DAYS MEMORIES

Those college days, I still remember,
The first day of it I hated it,
Because missed those school days always,
But then somehow got attached to it,
With those new crazy & stupid friends,
Who made me think college too can make us
cherish,
The feeling was something different because it felt
as if we had wings to fly,
Its campus always had a pleasant atmosphere,
With supporting professors who were as friendly as
those school teachers,
Those bunked lectures gave always bundle of joy
with some insane friends,
Miss those libraries that supported us with their
books,
The canteen fulfilled our stomach always whenever
we were hungry,
The gossip in the girl's room made us laugh,
Some of the crushes bloomed into love there,
Those different days that we celebrated made us
song & dance,
But one day those friends too parted just like those
school friends,
Yes, now I miss those college days too just like my
school days.

DIVYA DILIP SHETTY

THE NIGHT LISTENED

The night listened to my silence,
The crucial days and merciless nights,
When for no reason I had to face vice.
For diminishing the situation,
I had a voice that couldn't rise.
I was interrogated and seldom had any advice.
People started fearing my presence,
And started celebrating my absence.
I was put upon gender crisis and left in solitude,
There was nobody to hear the yelling inside me.
But then there was someone,
Who stood by me on that hour of violence,
Yes, the night listened to my silence.

MOHIT ANANDA

JOURNEY

It's been a long journey,
Mama says as she and I travel along the road,
She and I,
It's been like this for a very long time,
Yet I prefer it,
I prefer to have mama all to myself,
To laugh at her corny jokes,
To laugh as she says the most absurd things,
And mama knows they are absurd,
To call my crush her son in law is most absurd,
Yet she says it causes she knows it'll make me
laugh,
It'll make me smile,
Mama and nature are similar in that they both
bring me peace,
Both bring me warmth,
Both being a gift from the other;

I'm away from home today,
Away from the polluted city that brings me joy,
Away from busy streets filled with cars and
chattering people,
I sit amongst the mountains today,
Alone,
I look up at the stars as I often do at home,
It's a thing Dad and I did in the city,
Looking up,
Counting,
Until I got tired,
Yet the stars shine brighter here,
Perhaps cause the sky is clear,
Clear like how my heart becomes when I sit among
the trees,
As I listen to the crickets;

Crickets,
Strange how their voices don't scare me,
Strange how people's voices do,
Strange how I'm scared of society and its people yet
I'm not scared of the things they tell me to be afraid
of;

I see lights among the darkness of the night,
It reminds me of the life that I once lived,
A life I wish not to repeat,
A life that made me prefer immediate fear over the
lull of danger,
Mama says that a car is a weapon,
And she's right,
Nature has its weapons,
And so do people,
Yet nature doesn't use its weapons against itself"

SABENE RIZVI

<u>COLLEGE DAYS</u>

College days,
Thinking the vibes of my college days,
Morning to class and dozing every period,
As eyes say sleep first and class next...!!

Nicknames to last bench plays,
Cultural celebrations to love proposals,
Short term crushes to classroom blushes,
Project remarks to campus interviews...!!

If anyone makes any wrong,
We all sing the same song,
If anyone does any good,
We all stood in the same form!

Everything is fresh in our minds,
Wish that life would jump back,
Let's chat and laugh,
As before as college guys!

SUGNESWARAN S

THE COLOUR OF MY DREAMS

Every night I dream about a VIOLET garden,
I dream about RED cheeky children,
I dream about the big BLUE sky,
I dream about the WHITE clouds up high.
I dream about INDIGO flowers and GREEN grass,

I dream about VIOLET rivers and streams
stretching out vast,
I dream about listening to PINK and PURPLE
birds' hum mm,
I dream about YELLOW and ORANGE big bright
sun,
I wish that when I wake up, I see a world just like
that,
I wish to wake up a world that is worth looking at.

ARPITA KHARE

NOSTALGIC MEMORIES OF SCHOOL

Samosas in the canteen,
Festive like Halloween,
Turning desks into drums,
Bullet, every chalk becomes.
Balls of papers flying in the air,
Which my teacher didn't find fair.
Fighting around in gangs,
Still felt anyone's entry in pangs.
Assembly under the hot sun,
Still with peers was fun.
More than the ground, in our class, laid many balls,
Still gives energy, when it is recalled.
Class extended for hours,
Still did not feel any sour.
Now, things are not the same,
Everything happens for the sake of the name.

KALAIVANI UMAPATHY

TEENS LIFE

A crucial adolescent period of life,
Where college days, desire and many dreams lie;
Thirteen to nineteen is not just a number,
But a forming stage with different shades.
Many dreams are getting home, some desires to
forget,
College days are the backbone to build a life alike
building,
Age is like seventh teen season which is not
calculated but increasing.
Seasons come and go with changing time,
But the impression is like teens period very sharp.
College days are having summer vacation so as
winter exam,
So, teens have a da reams in every season with
colorful time.
Autumn leaves are showing after fall there is rise
again,
So as in teen's life leave some desires of dating and
fun.
Having big dreams of achievement and
accomplishments,
The adolescence of teen, a future of the nation, and
a bucket of full blossom flowers of parent's garden.

ROZY PAUL

VIRTUE OF OUR LOVE

On the brightest day,
In the darkest night,
A girl stays with me all her might,

On the brightest day,
In the darkest night,
Unsupported and alone I will give up,
I know there is no such fight,

On the brightest day,
In the darkest night,
If she isn't with me,
Sorry then at the end of the tunnel,
There might not even be any light,

In the darkest night,
On the brightest day,
I want her to be with me,
Just come with me.

NAVYA

COLLEGE LIFE- A LEARNING PHASE

"Entering Eighteenth With Childhood Gone;
Oh! Have to get up, it's my first college morn.

Funky clothes with a heart full of beaming screams;
I am here to meet my life's dream.

The young heart with magnificent aspirations;
Is still to meet its high expectations.

Life was not as easy as it was thought to be;
There were friends and flatterers too, you see.

Some moments were gaily and frolic;
Some were heartbreaking and melancholic.

Having learned the texts and lessons of life;
Stood up, built up, and heads for further strife."

PALAK VERMA

TRUE HAPPINESS WITHIN

Everything that God created in this world is
magnificent
Everything that exists and grows in nature is
resplendent

Denying the truth, felt withering like a flower
This is deprived of a hail shower
Craving to fulfill heart's desire
Yet willing to remain despair

With grief and desolation,
I glance at the beauty of nature
This is seen as perfect in its own nature
In the depth of heart, actualized my true nature
Convinced as precious to dream for bright future

From the lovely creation on earth
I gently ascertained, my own self worth
Which I lovingly embraced with warmth
Hence my inner soul obtained rebirth
Where true happiness is filled with

SUJATHA BALASWAMI

THE LOVE TO LIVE

Thou, the heart of my youthful body harks,
I wish to live a life full of holy nature;
But, my soul doth become fully dark,
With the fear on the wildest future.
I love to dream a life that is now unreal,
My youth hood doth need some magic;
From my ladylove to fill me with zeal,
Do thou need to attain a life with logic?
"Nay!" I say to myself when I get lost,
While I am seeking a path, I need to find;
The way to my success in a minute, fast,
My heart doth desire for the life in mind.
I have a love to live the unpredictable life,
My desire doth grow to get her to be my wife.

V. HEYMONTH KUMAR

WORDS

I rose up from my place,
Thinking of some writing space!
Wandering amidst of words;
Fancy and flavored one
Or subtle and simple pun.
To pull out my lost thoughts,
Where all these words got stuck!
Off! It goes flying and dancing
In each and every vacuum thought.
Pricking my soul, to dive deep –
Into the letters and words
Of the pages and book, I ever read!
Some may crack up your thought
Or some may even break up your heart,
But none got lost!
In this fancy dream of mine,
Building the intense bond of hope & trust,
Where I can sow and reap --
All these unborn words,
Without any aches and breaks
Filling and feeding
The scattered space of my mind,
In this Endless Wars of Life!

SHRUTHI ARAVINDAKSHAN

LOVABLE LYCEUM

Scintillating reminiscences of college days,
Stimulates a sense of sensitive susceptibility,
Educators eschew inscrutability wrapped in an
envelope of ignorance;
My heart being a reservoir of promises,
Never overflows or gets derelict;
I acclaim the echo of distant bound memories,
No scientist will ever be able to assess it,
The mystery hovers in unscrambling the emotional
enigma.

DR.V.ANURADHA

YOUTH'S DESIRE

Youth's desire is to aspire,
In their world of dreams to bonfire.
Intermixed with chaos and feelings,
Waking up with confidential promises and
aspiration,
Ending up with projects and assignments of their
institution.
Counting days of festivals and vacations,
To get rid from these burdensome situations.
In schools we are taught to become veracious,
Focus on your studies and be ambitious.
In colleges we are advised to be tenacious,
But we can't as we don't have any voracious aims,
Our moods and emotions fluctuate,
We messed up when we are trying to interrelate.
We interrogate within oneself,
Trying to figure out our goals and interests,
At last end up with parent's decision to circulate,
We hesitate and doubt on our potential,
It's hard for us to accept our failure,
Those who accept their flaws, they grow and lit up
their future with colors of success.

KOMAL JHA

CALLING FOR COLLEGE DAYS

Turning pages and greeneries,
Now they are just memories,
Dashing through open corridor,
Now I feel like an outsider.

Woke up late but right on time,
Spending money to the last dime,
Open pages and sleepy faces,
Winged birds escaping cages.

No mobile phones inside campus,
Online classes are just not for us,
The same old boring lectures,
But now they are happy pictures.

My good old times are college days,
Now meeting friends at coffee bays,
Oh, my golden days! No matter what anyone say.

POONGUZHALI.T

HARD TO BE GOOD!

Sometimes when I'm alone,
I cry because I am on my own;
The tears I cry are bitter and warm,
They flow with life but take no form.

I cry because my heart is torn,
And I find it difficult to carry on;
Have you ever loved someone so much
But they never understood?

When you were trying
So hard to be good!
I have tried so hard to
Make things work between us.

But some things are just a must,
You mean more than the world to me;
And now with someone else,
You will probably be.

Days I'll pick up the phone,
And give you a call.
Days I'm so sad I don't want,
To talk to you at all.

Can't tell you any more,
Where has love gone?
I'm torn once more
Thought you were the one

BHUMIKA

HELLO MY DEAR DIARY!

Hello my dear diary!

Memory is Strange, isn't it?
Some becomes a salty scare,
Many remain Mighty as Mountains,
Erasing is not at all easy task,
At the same time not tough too.
There was a Chair I used to stare,
The Black board scrolled me screenshot of
Allergic Algorithm, tricky trigonometry,
Yet I remembered the laughter lipstick,
I passed with pdf notes but the highlight is
I got gold medal with out of syllabus own stories.
Still, I remember we were in the final stage of
graduation
Yet we played hide and seek, rock paper
scissor, snake water gun like Kiddos.
Those are outstanding credit I can't give further
debit.
It's hard to conclude everything in single poem.
Isn't it?

P.KAVSHIKA (BARGAVI)

DREAMS ARE DESTINY

Walking in this world is not easy,
But my youth desired to stroll in the twilight.
Under the moonlit sky with the wind so breezy,
Gasping and heaving I reached the plight.
My dreams are not understandable but mysterious.
So, I asked the moon to lead me home.
People stopped my dreams, so serious.
But I danced under the moon, I feel like Sherlock
Holmes.
I love to choose and see my path,
Sing with birds and the English moor.
"Cease her dreams", they said with wrath.
But my youthful dreams shine even more.
My heart found a way.
My dreams are destined to stay.
This is what my youth desired today."

L. CAROLINE FELICITA

DESIRES OF YOUTH

Vivid dreams, innovative musings,
Wanting to master our thoughts;
Desires, crystal clear,
Our hopes stand higher.
Responsibilities, daring to comply,
When it's our time to fly!
Elapsing each day,
Hoping that our desires come true someday;
Dreams of a prudent life,
Whilst dealing with life's strife;
Heart high with hopes;
And for this,
We are ready to climb any ropes,
Never we are scared of slopes,
To accomplish our determined goals.

YAKATAA GS

LIFE ~ A CONFUSION

Many times, life brings us at such points,
When life itself becomes confusion.
But seems compulsory to be sure,
How to come out of that delusion.
People and needs in life are changed with time,
But the only thing is that we always want to shine.
We want to measure the heights of the sky, depths
of the ocean,
But unable to find the right direction.
The path we choose isn't approved by all,
Also have to face the names which people call.
Criticism will be always there for us, in one way or
the other.
But the point is that we don't have to bother.
So, choose the appropriate path and serve the duty.
Obey parents by the heart and help the needy.
Because People expecting your success and
happiness should never be hurt.

SONIYA SANGWAN

YOUTH'S DESIRE

The windy breeze soothed my bosom,
Heart waiting for my beloved one to confess,
The chirping of the birds makes me sing a song for
him,
My hands are trembling,
My eyes are blinking,
Yes, my lovable lad comes near me;
His eyes gazing at me,
My eyes are looking down to the earth,
He calls my name and suddenly my eyes lookup,
I saw his face,
He just glares at me simple look,
Suddenly, rain drizzles in my hand,
He holds my hand and makes me walk out of that
place and,
Makes me stand behind the tree,
That moment is my lovable moment, in my entire
life
He says, I just need to hold your hands throughout
my life
Suddenly, my eyes are full of tears
I just take another hand to my lovable hand."

ROSHINI.R

BACK TO THOSE DAYS

Remembering the days
When I set foot in to college
With vacant mind
Day one impels me diffident
Even so everything changes shortly
Our bond gets stronger
We mock at each other
Run away from the boring lecture
Great feast at college canteen
Passing through my crush
Makes me blush stupidly
Last day with teary eyes and
Huge hug cherished in me
Memories will live forever

KEERTHANA ARIVALAGAN

A HAPPY POET

I dreamt of being a happy poet
Whistling by the chaotic world;
Past the ire of dreary life
Admiring the azure above.
Young heart and soul so bright
With dreamy eyes and frisky smile.
I desired I could write away
Poems of an epic love of mine.

I dreamt of roving the ground below
With merry tunes awaiting a tale of love,
Amid the agile roses and petunias of life
I dreamt of being a poet of mirth.
Living a life of fancies and bloom
I was the heroine of my fictitious aeon.

ANWESA MAIT

DESIRE GETS WINGS TO ASPIRE

Hey, you are growing
Just as love of mine
You know what the heart desire is
We sit near a campfire
The light of trust
Hands on Hands without wine or lust
Where spreading dignity
And clearing the dust
You know what the heart desire is
To fly as cloud that is higher
To rain down over the earth
And to feel the love and the girth
Now, just getting active around the meth
In dream kissing you out the breath.

RPH SUMITA NATH

COLLEGE DAYS

Can't hold the memories up in the brain,
But deep down in the heart!
Can't remember the lesson in the books,
But can't forget the lesson for life!
Can't decide if I want to visit the campus,
But always run to my best friend's place!
Can't believe the time ran so fast forward,
But the heart still has that blast!
Can't control the flow of life in the present,
But absorb energy from the golden past!
Can't deny the fact that we all are different,
But always come together for us!
Can't convey the thanks for their time,
But always grateful for God for giving College days
as a blessing!

JUVAHIR BEGUM

COLLEGE LIFE

Recollecting those days,
Cherishes my mind,
Lasting forever,
Full of memories,
Surrounded by many friends,
Happiness is what we know,
And nothing more.
Working hard to score,
Reaching our goal,
Was not easy,
Listening to lectures,
Making and taking notes,
Humble and sincere,
In all works we do.
Our college,
Thought us to build,
A good society,
Being an example,
That is what it gave.

DR. M. KANIKA PRIYA

GOOD DREAM

Woke up, went for a jog,
In the midst of the fog,
Refreshed and came for eating
While my mom served me and my family
She asked about my plans today
And I told her it's a big day
Because I'm making big decisions
Without any of her concessions
That is, I am working there for three years,
Indeed, gonna resign in spite of all my fears.
Thought of starting a business,
And prove everyone as a witness.
It was a big rough day though
Had a great time with pending files
Went home and got fresh up
When I sat down at the table,
And shouted to an employee in a call,
My mom came near me and shook
And then I woke up,
She asked for a bad dream
I said, a good dream,
That I missed in reality.

JAYALAKSHMI S

A PART OF MY LIFE

It is the day that changes every student's future as said, my mother. If you complete this, you need not any more struggle in your life, say all parents: any clue?? Actually, it is +2 examinations that all parents lecture about...

While we enter the tenth grade, they shall start singing "study, study, study". If it is a lion to deal with. Twelfth grade is a hyena to be sacred of. Besides the result day is like a student must be ready to tackle the situation where all cages in a zoo are opened.

The very day came in my life; it was the result day that day. The terrible night I had had the previous day. I was uptight all night worrying about my marks, my friend's score, and my parents' reactions. By 7 am on television every news channel's first headline was "HSC results will be declared sharply at 10.00 am and students can check out their results on the official website and from schools SMS will be sent to you. Watching the news my heart started fluttering, my face beautifully revealed nervousness and fear.

The mobile did glow; I tiptoed to check if it was for me. Mom said, "Hey wait, I will check it out". With a surprised reaction, mom congratulated me saying "You have scored 90%". I was on cloud nine. My racing heart pumped even more blood but now in excitement.

The next segment was engineering counseling in Anna University Chennai. Fresh morning in spring season; the trees in University bloomed with beautiful red Gulmohar flowers, leafy neem tree, peepul trees, and many more and huge in the count. Admiring the surrounding I got exclaimed seeing numerous engineering aspirants queued before me happily. Lucky people had got a seat in their favorite college. And I was one of those.

September 9, 2008, was my first day of college. I put on my orange chudidar and hung my dupatta with some folds on my left shoulder. I entered the first-year computer science classroom where already many new students like me were in. Looking at new girls' and boys' faces eyeing me I felt uneasy and nerve-wracking event in my body disturbed my calm stomach and butterflies, and of course, cockroaches were flying in.

Months left, I made new friends, learned new things. First-semester result in which I cleared all papers with 72%. I became familiar with the friends' circle from that day. We all exchanged mobile numbers. Our frequent chats in our 1600 Nokia mobile, sharing lunch between friends, assignment writing for our friends made college life wonderful. Though I had many good friends, I had a bestie who corrected my mistakes, helped me develop, and appreciated my qualities.

One of the best moments we had in our industrial visit to Infosys, Mysore where we visited many other places like palaces, parks. Talking during bus travel with friends and photographs remarked our happiness.

Three years left very fast. The most important time I was in. That was a campus interview. Two days of the interview went on. After successful completion of written, GD, Technical rounds, I was welcomed to the final round and that was a personal interview in a big room where a tall, thin, man with a French beard in a black coat suit shot me with many questions to test my presence of mind, language skill and personality development. I had managed to answer all his questions with my knowledge and mock interviews I attended in college helped me that time. When the pool campus was over, it was almost night I waited for the result again. All selected members were called and issued offer letters. As shown in the movie, till the last minute I was kept tense and finally, they announced "S.Kirubavathi". Happy tears rolled down; hands were trembling in excitement.

When I received the offer letter, I thanked God for accomplishing my dream. An immediate call to my dad who was in the hospital delighted him and my family. Hugs and wishes from my friends made my day.

I successfully completed my course in 2012. Standing before parents in graduation cap and Gown is every child and their parents' dream and I made it.

KIRUBAVATHI S

55